I AM READING

JOE LION'S BIG BOOTS

KARA MAY

ILLUSTRATED BY

JONATHAN ALLEN

ER

To Marian & Isobel
& Alasdair—J. A.

KINGFISHER
a Houghton Mifflin Company imprint
222 Berkeley Street
Boston, Massachusetts 02116
www.houghtonmifflinbooks.com

First published by Kingfisher in 2000
This edition published in 2005
2 4 6 8 10 9 7 5 3 1
1TR/0904/AJT/RNB(SACH)/115MA/F

LIBRARY OF CONGRESS CATALOGING-IN-PUBLICATION DATA
May, Kara.
Joe Lion's big boots/by Kara May ; illustrated by Jonathan Allen.—1st ed.
p. cm.—(I am reading)
Summary: Joe Lion, desperate to get bigger, acquires a
pair of boots that make him taller, but he soon finds that they
bring certain disadvantages and that he prefers being himself.
[1. Size—Fiction. 2. Boots—Fiction. 3. Self-acceptance—Fiction.
4. Lions—Fiction.] I. Allen, Jonathan, ill. II. Title. III. Series
PZ7.M4524 Jo 2000
[E]—dc21
00-22567

ISBN 0-7534-5856-X
ISBN 978-07534-5856-3

Printed in India

Contents

Chapter One

Joe Lion was small.

He was the smallest in his class.

He couldn't even reach the goldfish to feed it.

"It's only me who can't reach," said Joe.

He was the smallest in his family, too.
Big Brother Ben could reach
the cookie jar, easy as pie.
Sister Susan could reach it too.
But Joe? He couldn't reach it,
not even on tiptoe.

"I'm tired of being small,"

he said to Mom and Dad.

"I was small once," said Dad.

"You'll grow bigger one day,"

Mom told him.

But Joe wanted to be bigger NOW.

"I'll WISH myself bigger," he said.

He closed his eyes and wished.

He was still wishing when

he went to bed.

But the next morning he was

the same small Joe Lion.

"Wishing hasn't made me bigger," he said.

"I'll have to think of something else."

He went to the big, comfy chair

where he did his thinking.

But what was on the chair?

It was Mom's new book,

How to Grow Sunflowers.

"Aha!" grinned Joe.

"That gives me an idea."

Big Brother Ben had a *How to . . .*

book—just the book Joe wanted.

He raced up to Ben's room.

On the bed he saw the book:

How to Build Yourself a Bigger Body.

KEEP OUT!
HOW TO BUILD YOURSELF A BIGGER BODY

Joe read through it in a flash.

To get bigger, he had to eat

lots of food like pasta.

Mmm! Yum!

"I have to work out, too," said Joe.

"I know where I can do that!"

Chapter Two

Joe ran all the way to Gus Gorilla's gym.

Gus was big. Very big!

"Working out seems to do the trick,"

thought Joe.

"I can't wait to start," he said to Gus.

"What do I have to do?"

"You stand on this and run!" said Gus.

Joe ran on the treadmill.

Then it was on to the exercise bike.

After that it was the rowing machine.

"Now, lift these weights, young Joe," said Gus. "Lift them good and high."

Joe's arms ached. His legs ached.

Even his little finger ached!

But he wanted to be bigger.

He picked up the weights.

He lifted them good and high . . .

until a weight fell—

“Yikes! It almost hit my foot. That’s the end of working out for me,” said Joe.

But he was still determined to get bigger.

“Now that I’m not working out,” said Joe, “I’ll do lots of extra eating to make up for it.” Wherever Joe went, whatever Joe was doing, it was: MUNCH! CRUNCH! GOBBLE!

At home:

At school:

On the bus:

MUNCH! CRUNCH! GOBBLE!

Even in the bathtub:

MUNCH! CRUNCH! GOBBLE!

"I must be bigger by now,"
said Joe at last. He went to
take a look in the mirror.
He didn't like what he saw.
"Oh no," he groaned. After
all that working out and
eating, he was bigger, yes.
Bigger-WIDER!

"But I want to be bigger-TALLER!"
said Joe.
Sister Susan had gotten bigger-taller
in only five minutes.
He asked her how she did it.
"I put on my high-heeled shoes,"
she said.
"Aha!" said Joe.
"That gives me an idea . . . !"

Chapter Three

Joe rushed into Ernie Elephant's shoe store.

"I need some shoes to make me bigger-taller," he said.

"Boots are best for that," said Ernie.

Joe tried on lots of boots, but none of them made him as bigger-taller as he wanted.

"I can make you some," said Ernie.
"But it'll cost you, AND you have
to pay in advance."
Joe paid Ernie. "It's all the money
I have, but it will be worth it,"
said Joe.
"I'll bring them over to you—
delivery is free," said Ernie.

Joe couldn't wait
for the new boots
to arrive.
But at last, here was
Ernie. Now for the
BIG MOMENT.

Joe took the lid off the box.
He took out his new boots and
put them on.
"This is more like it!" said Joe.
He went to show the others.
"Surprise, surprise!
I'm a lot bigger-taller now."
They were surprised, all right—
too surprised to speak!

Bigger-taller Joe could do lots of things that he couldn't do before.

He could reach the hall light. He turned it on and off—just because he could!

He could reach the rope to swing from.

He could see over Gus Gorilla's fence.

His new boots made a great noise, too!

CLOMP! CLOMP! CLOMP!

"I'll call them my Clomping Clompers," said Joe.

"That's a good name for them," said Mom.

But the next morning Mom said, "You can't wear those things to school!"

"I *have* to wear them," said Joe.

In his Clomping Clompers he wouldn't be the smallest in the class.

"I feel like an ant that's turned into a giant," he said as he set off for school.

Today was going to be his best school day ever!

Chapter Four

Joe made his way to the bus stop.

"I like this bigger-taller me!"

he said.

He was closer to the

sky, and he could

feel the sun better.

He saw the bus coming
and ran to catch it—or tried to!
In his Clomping Clompers he could
only: CLOMP! CLOMP! CLOMP!

The bus left without him.

Joe was late for school.

Mrs. Croc wasn't pleased.

"I'm sorry, Mrs. Croc," said Joe.

"It was my Clomping Clompers."

"May I feed the goldfish?" he asked.

But the goldfish was already fed.

At recess his friends were playing soccer. Joe was good at scoring goals.

But not in his Clomping Clompers.

Joe was glad to get home.

"Cookie jar, here I come!"

He reached it, easy as pie.

Next he wanted to watch his favorite TV show, *Super Lion in Space*.

But then Mom said, "Hang up your coat, Joe. You can reach the hook in your Clomping Clompers."

And that was just the start of it.

Joe could reach lots of things that he couldn't reach when he was small Joe Lion.
Like the kitchen sink:
"Now you can wash the dishes," said Big Brother Ben.

Like the toy shelf:

"You can put your toys up there yourself," said Sister Susan.

Doing the dishes! Cleaning up!

"It's all I seem to do these days!" said Joe.

But he couldn't do much else in his Clomping Clompers.

Later Joe's friends were going to the park.

"Are you coming, Joe?" they asked.

Joe shook his head.

He couldn't join in the games.

"I can only clomp!" he said.

"I'm going for a walk."

Joe clomped off down the street.

CLOMP! CLOMP! CLOMP!

But what was up with Jeff Giraffe?

"He looks like he's in trouble!"

said Joe.

Chapter Five

Joe soon discovered that Jeff
WAS in trouble.
"Silly giraffe that I am,
I've locked myself out," he said.
"I came outside to pick some flowers,
and I left the water running!"
Joe saw the problem right away.
Left alone, the bathtub would overflow,
and Jeff's house would be flooded!

Joe spotted the bathroom window—
it was open!
"You can get in up there," he said.
Jeff pushed his head through the window.

"But my bottom half won't fit,"
said Jeff. "The window's too small."
"Leave it to me," said Joe.

He knew what he had to do.
First, off with his Clomping
Clompers.

Then it was
Super Joe Lion
to the rescue!
Up the drainpipe.
In through the
window.

The water was rising fast—
along with lots of soapy bubbles!
“I have to do something!” Joe reached
for the plug.

It was too far down.

He would have to go in!

He got up on the side of the bathtub and jumped.

He couldn't see through the bubbles,

and he was having trouble breathing.

But he had to get to the plug.

"Got it!" He pulled the plug, and

out it came.

The water gurgled down.

GLUG! GLUG! GLUG!

Joe whooshed the bubbles

out the window.

Then he slid back down
the drainpipe.
He saw that a crowd had gathered.
Mom and Dad were there—and
Brother Ben and Sister Susan
and Gus and Ernie and
Mrs. Croc and all his friends.
They were waiting for news.

Quickly, Joe told them:

"Jeff's house is safe from flooding bathwater, and it's safe from bubbles, too!"

They all cheered.

"Hooray for Super Joe Lion!"

Joe felt very proud.

He was Super Joe Lion—just the way he was. He didn't need his Clomping Clompers.

"My clomping days are over," said Joe. "Being me is best. I don't want to be bigger . . . well, not yet!"

About the author and illustrator

Kara May was born in Australia, and as a child she acted on the radio. She says, "Even though I am grown-up now, I am still the smallest in my family, so I know just how Joe Lion feels." Kara used to work in the theater and has written many plays for children, but now she writes books full-time.

Jonathan Allen played bass guitar in a band before he graduated from art school. He says, "When I was young, I wanted to be a famous rock star, like the one in the poster on Brother Ben's bedroom wall." Now Jonathan is well-known for illustrating children's books . . . but he does still play his bass guitar!

Strategies for Independent Readers

Predict

Think about the cover, illustrations, and the title of the book. What do you think this book will be about? While you are reading think about what may happen next and why.

Monitor

As you read ask yourself if what you're reading makes sense. If it doesn't, reread, look at the illustrations, or read ahead.

Question

Ask yourself questions about important ideas in the story such as what the characters might do or what you might learn.

Phonics

If there is a word that you do not know, look carefully at the letters, sounds, and word parts that you do know. Blend the sounds to read the word. Ask yourself if this is a word you know. Does it make sense in the sentence?

Summarize

Think about the characters, the setting where the story takes place, and the problem the characters faced in the story. Tell the important ideas in the beginning, middle, and end of the story.

Evaluate

Ask yourself questions like: Did you like the story? Why or why not? How did the author make the story come alive? How did the author make the story fun to read? How well did you understand the story? Maybe you can understand it better if you read it again!